MY KINDERGARTEN

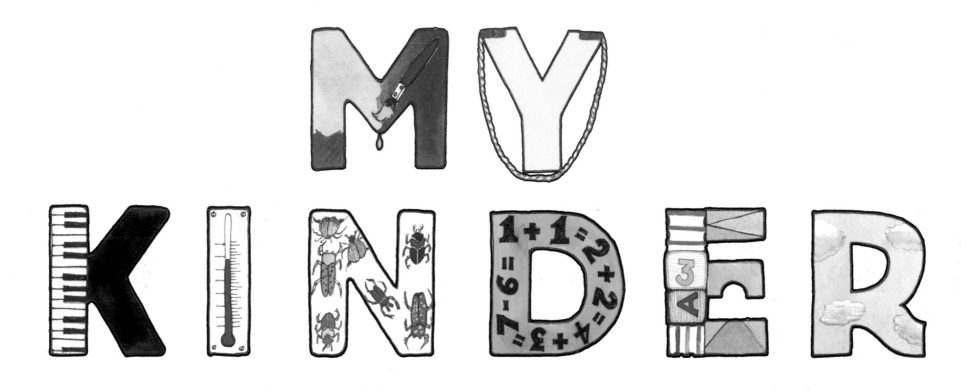

MY KINDER

Diane Duck

LOUISE

OTTO

Emily

GARTEN

Rosemary Wells

HYPERION BOOKS FOR CHILDREN

NEW YORK

To Ed Spicer,
my Teacher of the Year

Text and illustrations copyright © 2004 by Rosemary Wells
114 Fifth Avenue, New York, New York 10011.
Printed in Singapore
First Edition
1 3 5 7 9 10 8 6 4 2
Reinforced binding
This book is set in Pabst
ISBN 0-7868-0833-0

Visit www.hyperionbooksforchildren.com

INTRODUCTION

IF YOU FOUND YOURSELF on a desert island with a kindergartner and only one book, this is the book to have. Every mother and dad wants their child to succeed in school. *My Kindergarten* is the place to start. Use this book to involve your child in math, science, language, community, music, art, and holidays. Every topic leads to learning activities that are fun and worthwhile. For example, "Weeds and Seeds" inspires parents and children to collect their own seed pods and identify leaves; "Geography" shows kindergartners how they can make their own maps of their homes and neighborhoods while they explore their worlds.

When I was a kindergarten teacher, I found my children liked to have me read the same poems over and over until they could say the rhymes along with me. They knew the poems inside and out. They took turns pointing to the words as we repeated them. They were learning to read. Rosemary Wells sprinkles numerous rhymes, songs, and poems throughout *My Kindergarten*. Each one offers an opportunity to help your child learn to read and to enjoy reading.

My Kindergarten provides unlimited opportunities to connect what kindergartners do at home with what they do every day in kindergarten. It's a book I wish I'd had when I was teaching and when I was raising my own children. Enjoy every page you turn, and explore the exciting world of kindergarten together.

Bernice Cullinan, Ph.D.
Professor Emeritus, New York University

CONTENTS

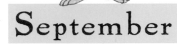

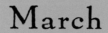

The Night Before the First Day of School

Tomorrow is the first day
of kindergarten.
What will I do? What will it be like?
Everything will be for the first time!
I tell Mama I am scared to go.
We sing our favorite song:

> *Star light, star bright,*
>
> *First star I see tonight,*
>
> *I wish I may, I wish I might*
>
> *Have the wish I wish tonight.*

"You are my little star," says Mama.

The First Day of School

On the first day of school I meet
Miss Cribbage, our teacher.
She says hello to each of us by name.
How does she know our names?
"That's my secret!" says Miss Cribbage.
She asks us, "Boys and girls, what is today?"
"The first day of school," answers everyone.

"What does the word *first* mean?"
asks Miss Cribbage.
Louise raises her hand.
"We have never been in school before today,"
says Louise. "After today, it will never be
the first day again."
"I won first prize in the sweet-corn-eating contest," says Diane Duck.
Then and there, I decide Diane Duck will be my first friend.

Getting to Ten

Diane Duck and I help each other
with our number songs.

Miss Cribbage gave Diane "Four." I have "Six."

One for the money,
  two for the show.
Three to get ready, and
  four to go!

One, two, three, and
  four, five, six.
All good children
  pick up sticks!

When Diane Duck stays over at my house

we sing everyone's number songs.

Mama turns out our light. We still sing under the covers until

Papa says we absolutely, definitely, totally have to go to sleep.

Word for the Week

Miss Cribbage says every week she will give us a new "Word for the Week." We will make a word board, where we will collect all our important words. This week, the word is *and*. "What other words start with the letter *A*?" she asks.

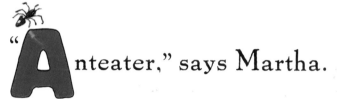 "**A**nteater," says Martha.

 "**A**ir," says Odysseus.

"**A**che-y break-y heart!" says Louise.

Roger writes his *A* upside down. "He is allowed to write it any way he likes," says Miss Cribbage.

Zigs and Zags

We all wear different clothes.
What are these patterns and designs called?
Do they have names?
"Yes, they do," says Miss Cribbage.

Calico

Tweed

Polka Dots

Zig Zags

Paisley

Stripes

Checks

Plaid

Automobiles

We Did It All for You!

"Who comes to Back to School Night?" asks Miss Cribbage.

"Everyone's family comes!" we say.

We are so proud.

The school bus is ready to pick up families who live far away.

The sixth grade is ready to babysit the babies.

Otto makes paper autumn leaves for our classroom windows.

Diane Duck makes name cards.

I stamp the invitations.

Miss Cribbage mails them.

I can't wait for Mama and Papa
to open their invitation.

When they do, I say, "Look! Look!

I stamped it myself! Please, please come!"

"We wouldn't miss it for the world!" they say.

burdock burrs

milkweed pods

pokeweed pods

curly dock seeds

cattail

Weeds and Seeds

Odysseus is my Weeds and Seeds partner.

At recess, we collect fall seeds in little bags.

We will make a Weeds and Seeds chart for the science corner.

Odysseus loves milkweed pods.

We go to Odysseus's house for lunch.

Odysseus's mama makes us lemon soup.

Odysseus's papa plays on his special guitar

called a bouzouki. He sings:

The lining of a milkweed pod is
*   as soft as my mother's hair.*
As soft as a kitten's tummy,
As soft as the summer air.

18

ACORNS · MAPLE WINGS · BLACK WALNUTS

BURDOCK BURRS · CATTAIL FLUFF · PIGWEED

PINECONES · GRASS SEED · SUNFLOWER

SEEDS · ROSE HIPS · MILKWEED PODS

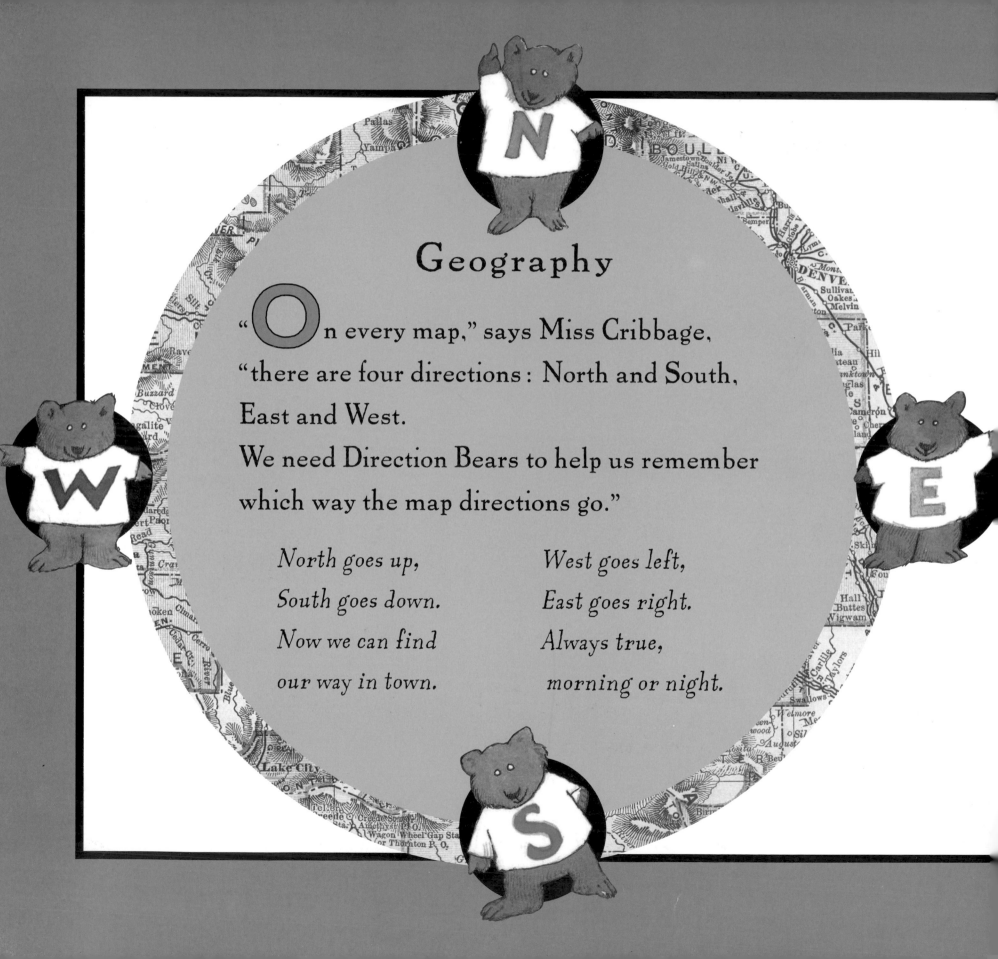

Geography

"On every map," says Miss Cribbage, "there are four directions: North and South, East and West.

We need Direction Bears to help us remember which way the map directions go."

North goes up,
South goes down.
Now we can find
our way in town.

West goes left,
East goes right.
Always true,
morning or night.

Miss Cribbage helps us draw a map of our classroom.

Music 1
Science 2
Art 3
Cleanup 4
Blocks 5
Dress-up 6
Reading 7
Desks 8

E Emily
D Diane Duck
O Otto
R Roger
L Louise
O Odysseus
T Terrance
M Martha
Miss Cribbage

Our Classroom

"Now, let's go outside the classroom!"
says Miss Cribbage.

Our classroom in our school

We draw a map of Cranberry Island School.

On the east side are the boys' and girls' rooms and our classroom.

On the west side are the other grades.

All the rooms in the school are easy to find.

Next we make a map of our school in our town.
Our school is on the east side
of the map of Cranberry Island.

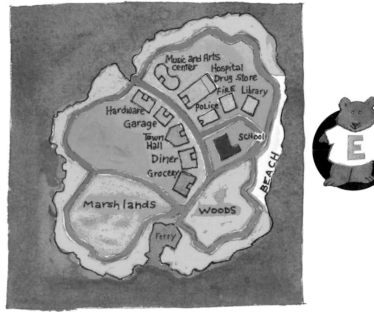

Our school in our town

Our town in our state

We draw the rest of the state of Maine.
Maine is to the west of Cranberry
Island.

The state of Maine is very far north and very far east in the United States. Miss Cribbage colors it red so we can all see it. If you look closely you will see tiny Cranberry Island off the coast, in the bright blue sea.

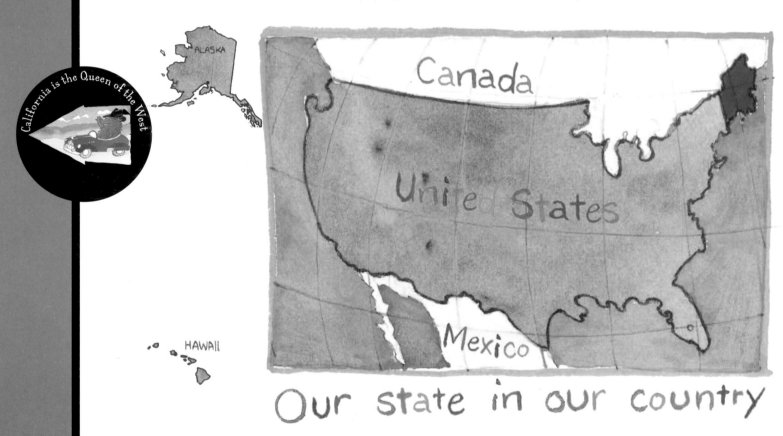

Our state in our country

Over the Ocean Blue

On Columbus Day I tell my family about Columbus's voyage.

"How far did he go?" asks my brother, Leo.

"A hundred days and nights in a squeaky, leaky boat," I say.

"He sailed from Spain to the New World over the ocean blue."

I draw a map of the trip with carrots right on the table.

Then I sing the rhyme we learned in school:

In fourteen hundred and ninety-two,
Columbus sailed the ocean blue.

Rainbow Fruits

Diane Duck has the Juice Pourer's job.

How can Diane tell what kind of juice is inside each box?

"I can read the picture on the label!" says Diane Duck.

We all bring in our favorite juice labels.

Diane Duck brings in a bug juice label.

"Miss Cribbage might get mad," I say to Diane Duck.

But Miss Cribbage does not get mad.

Why We Have Halloween

"**W**hy do we have Halloween?" I ask.

"Because," says Granny, "in the old days ghosts came out one night a year and flew around, making trouble.

So everyone carved pumpkins into faces to scare them away.

It was called All Hallows' Eve," says Granny.

After supper, we light our jack-o'-lantern candle.

I can almost see the ghosts and pumpkins, and hear the hoot owls hooting, from a hundred years ago.

Our Tree

What will we call the
schoolyard tree?
Otto has an idea.
"Doris O'Maple" seems right to us all.
She's ours for the rest of the year.

Doris O'Maple's a beautiful tree.
Her leaves have turned yellow and red.
I sit on her branch and pretend
     I'm in France.
The colors have
     gone to my head.

Here is our tree in November.
I sit in her highest-up fork.
Her leaves are all blown to
     places unknown.
I can see all the way to New York.

Doris O'Maple loves winter.
Her branches are covered with ice.
They snap and they tap
     on the windowpane,
Like hundreds of scampering mice.

Doris O'Maple wakes up in the spring
After her long winter's nap.
She gives us a spoonful of syrup a day,
Made from her sugary sap.

Doris O'Maple puts on her new dress
With delicate yellowy sleeves.
She twirls out samaras all
     over the grass,
And then puts on serious leaves.

Fall

winter

spring

summer

X-tras for Everyone

Our alphabet party is ready.
But no one can think of something to eat beginning
with the letter X.
Finally, Odysseus has an idea.
"How about X-tras for Everyone!" says Odysseus.

African Avocado
with Almonds

Baked Banana

Cherry Cobbler

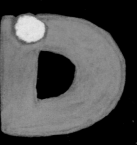

Deviled
Dandelion

Eggplant
Enchiladas

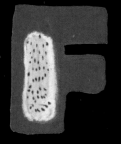

Figs
Fricassee

Gingered
Grapes

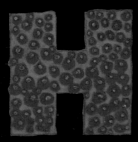

Huckleberries
and Honey

Irish Ice

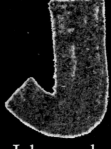

Johnnycakes
with Jam

Kiwi Kebabs

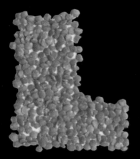
Lentil
Ladyfingers

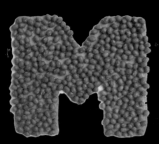
Mung Bean
Muffins

Nectarine Noodles
with Nutmeg

Orange Omelet

Pepita Pie

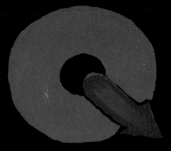
Quick
Quesadillas

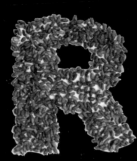
Risotto
with Rhubarb

Strawberry
Salad

Tomato Tacos

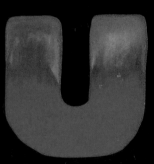
Unsurpassed
Ugli fruit

Vanilla Ice Cream

Watermelon
Waffles

X-tras for Everyone

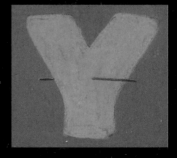
Yam Yakitori

Zebra Zabaglione

Our Horizons

"At Choice Time we will widen our horizons," says Miss Cribbage.

Each day I try something new.

So does Diane Duck.

Roger stays in the car-and-truck corner.

He does not want to build blocks,

or dress up, or paint.

Roger does not go near the science table.

Roger makes gearshift noises and

says words like "generator."

"Roger is not widening his horizons,"

says Diane Duck.

"It takes all kinds to make a world," says Miss Cribbage.

Choice Time

Martha measures her feet.

Otto plays a scale.

Louise scores a goal.

Terrance builds a tower.

Ithaca Ughs

Grandpa takes us to a Tigers football game.
How can all these people know the Tigers' song?
"It rhymes!" says Grandpa.
"Everything that rhymes is easy to remember."
He sings it once, and then we sing it together.
The third time I know all the words by heart.

We root for the Down East Tigers.
They're beating the Ithaca Ughs.
The air is cold, but our cocoa is warm
And we're wrapped in buffalo rugs.
Hooray, for the Down East Tigers!
We yell it out loud and clear.

"Ugh! Ugh! Ugh!" shouts the other side
Because that's the Ithaca cheer.
Down in the dells from far and near
Echoes and swells the Ithaca cheer,
"Ugh! Ugh! Ugh! Ithaca's here!"

Being Thankful

Miss Cribbage says, "We are all thankful for something. Draw a picture of your favorite thing in the world that you are thankful for!"

Roger is thankful for blue convertibles.

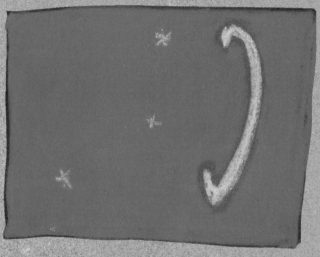

Martha is thankful for the moon and stars.

Louise is thankful for lobster.

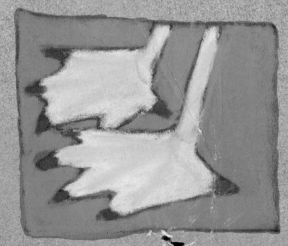

Diane Duck is thankful for red nail polish.

Otto is thankful for music.

Terrance is thankful for baseball.

Odysseus is thankful
for lemon soup.

Emily is thankful for snow.

All along, Miss Cribbage has been drawing, too.
"I am most thankful for all of you!" says Miss Cribbage.

Singing a Song

"We will learn a Christmas song," says Miss Cribbage.
The song is in a very old language called Latin.
The words mean "Give us peace."

Dona Nobis Pacem

Festival of Lights

"Today is the last day of Hanukkah," says Miss Cribbage.

Miss Cribbage lights our menorah.

We eat our potato pancakes.

We sing Hebrew words to our peace song.

"Where shall we aim the song?" asks Miss Cribbage.

We aim our peace song in the direction of trouble and sing loud.

We hope all the children who need peace can hear us far away.

Kwanzaa

We mix flour and water and shredded newspapers to make a papier-mâché cup and candleholder for Kwanzaa. We paint them red, black, and green, the colors of Kwanzaa.

"Kwanzaa" means 'first fruits' in Swahili," says Miss Cribbage.

"Swahili is a language spoken in parts of Africa."

Otto finds Africa on the world map. We sing our peace song in Swahili.

Oo tu pay amani means "Peace on earth."

We sing loud, through the open windows, so that children far away in all the countries of Africa can hear our song.

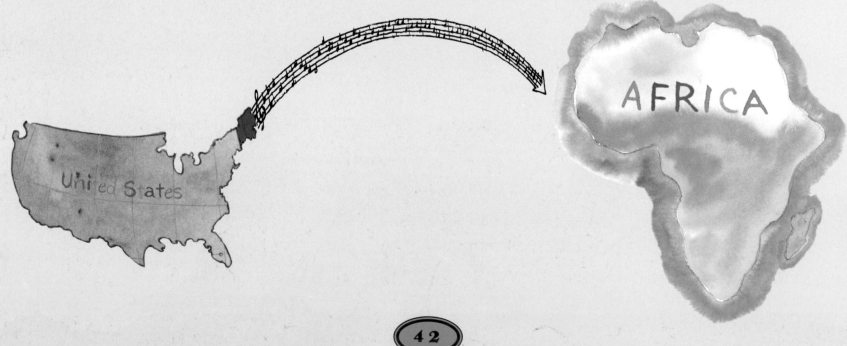

Our Christmas Gifts

We stuff stockings for children who are not
as lucky as the children of Cranberry Island, Maine.
In my stocking goes a chocolate Santa, a pair of warm socks, and
a harmonica. On Christmas Eve, a plane flies far above our house
against the silver moon.

"That may be the very plane
carrying your stocking,"
 says Mama.
"Who will get it? Will they sing
and dance?" I ask.
"Oh yes," Mama says to me,
"so you sing and dance back!"

I Won't Dance

Miss Cribbage plays bluegrass dance music.

Martha cannot follow the square-dance steps.

She gets them wrong every time.

Everyone has to stop for Martha.

This makes Martha cry.

"Do you like the music, Martha?" asks Miss Cribbage.

"Yes!" says Martha. "But I won't dance."

"While we dance," says Miss Cribbage,

"why don't you make us a picture of the music?"

Martha draws a picture of blue, blue grass.

Colors of Winter

"The winter is colored boring gray," says Diane Duck.

"But, look!" I say.

"There is a bright red scarf walking by on the street.

There are bright red boots and a green hat and a purple umbrella."

Diane looks out.

"Orange is the color of the snowplow," she says,

"and blue is the color of the policeman's uniform."

Winter is just as bright as summer, but in different places.

African Stamps

Terrance has stamps from Ireland.

They have harps on them.

We paste them on the world map.

Louise has stamps from France.

But I have none.

Then, suddenly, on a very ordinary cloudy

Tuesday afternoon, a package arrives, too big to fit

 inside the mailbox.

It comes from Africa, where my uncle Harry is visiting.

In the package are African beach shells for Eloise,

African bird feathers for me,

and African stones for Leo.

But, oh—those African stamps!

The Power of Love

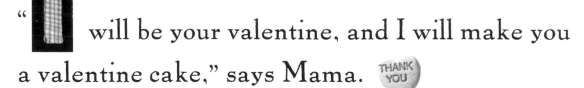

"**I** will be your valentine, and I will make you
a valentine cake," says Mama.

"Then you will be my valentine too."

She gets out the once-a-year heart-shaped pan.

The late-afternoon wind blows snow against

the kitchen windowpane.

It howls down the chimney of our house.

It makes the trees chatter.

"What keeps winter outside?" I ask.

"We are valentines," says Mama.

"The power of love is warmer than any snow

or ice in the world."

Grown-ups Vote

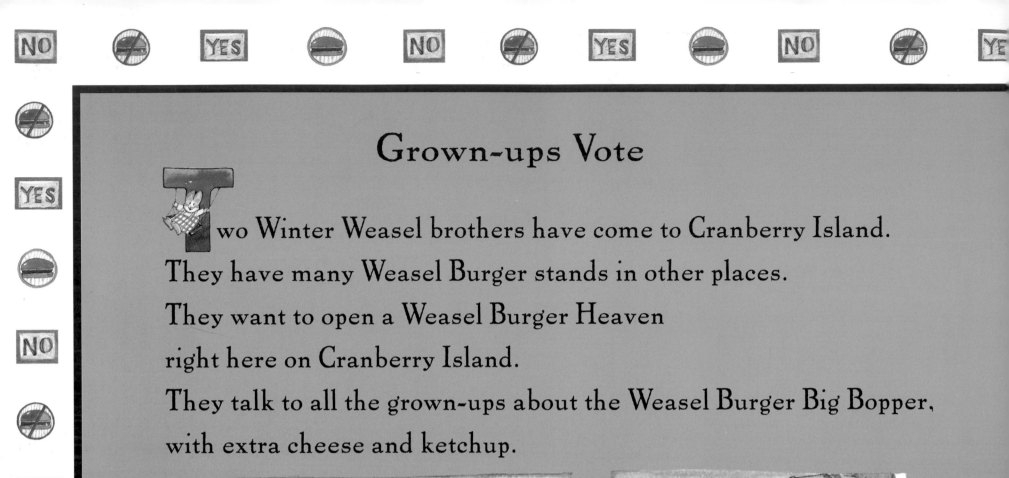

Two Winter Weasel brothers have come to Cranberry Island.

They have many Weasel Burger stands in other places.

They want to open a Weasel Burger Heaven

right here on Cranberry Island.

They talk to all the grown-ups about the Weasel Burger Big Bopper,

with extra cheese and ketchup.

My papa says, "A Weasel Burger Heaven will put

Dorothy's sandwich shop out of business.

Dorothy is our neighbor. We want to support her."

My mama says Weasel Burger wrappers make a lot of litter.

Weasel Burgers are not good for anyone, anyway.

It is up to the people who live here to say Yes, they want a

Weasel Burger Heaven, or No, we don't.

In class we vote on which story we want.

The grown-ups vote, too.

The grown-ups' votes are put on ballots.

The ballots are counted.

Not many Cranberry Islanders want
a Weasel Burger Heaven on
Cranberry Island.

The Weasel brothers leave town
in a huff.

Dorothy makes them bean sprout
sandwiches and waves good-bye from
the ferry dock.

"We vote," says Grandpa, "in order to try
and make more good things than bad
things happen in our world."

Plain Speaking

"I draw good," says my brother, Leo.

"No, Leo," says Papa. "You must not say, 'I draw good.'

You say, 'I draw well.' It's important!" says Papa.

"Why?" asks Leo.

Papa gets up and blows Eloise's trombone.

He blows a big, loud, terrible blast.

"That sounds like needles in swamp water!"

says Leo.

Papa hands the trombone to Eloise.

She plays us a song.

"That sounds terrific!" says Leo.

"When you use the right words," says Papa,

"our language is beautiful to hear.

The words are precious.

They need care, like your

crayons or my baseball glove."

What's-It-Made-of? Boxes

Terrance gives Miss Cribbage a pencil stub.

It goes into our What's-it-made-of? boxes.

The pencil stub is vegetable and mineral.

It's vegetable because part of it is made

of wood and rubber.

It's also mineral. It has graphite and a metal eraser holder.

Everyone brings something to put in the boxes.

Each thing gets its label.

Soon we have the Museum of Things.

Soon we know what everything in the world is made of.

animal   mineral   vegetable

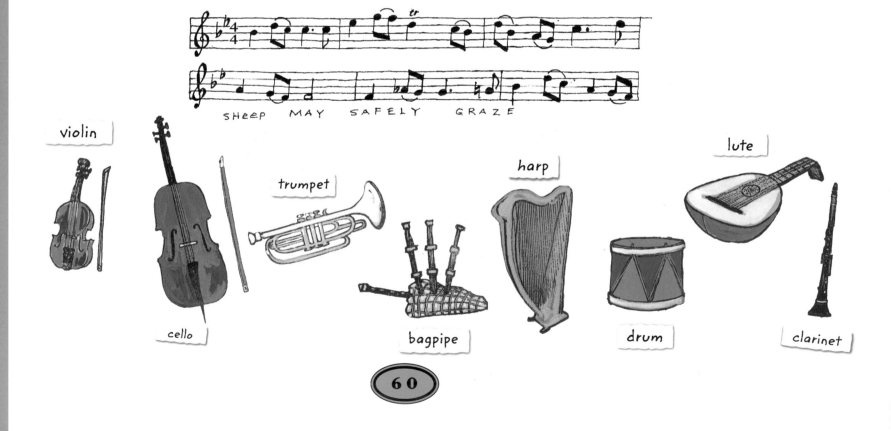

Song for the Day

Miss Cribbage plays us ten minutes of music every morning.

"If anybody's feet are wet, or they didn't sleep well, or they are in a bad mood, music will make it all better," says Miss Cribbage.

Music does. Sometimes the music is clear and twinkly. Other times, it is swoony or hoppy.

Today's music is called "Sheep May Safely Graze."

SHEEP MAY SAFELY GRAZE

violin

trumpet

harp

lute

cello

bagpipe

drum

clarinet

Math Crash

Miss Cribbage asks me to write the number 95 on the board.

I can't do it.

Odysseus writes it instead.

I begin to cry. I have forgotten what every single number looks like.

Diane Duck and Louise sit with me until I stop crying.

"I do not want there to be any more numbers.

There are too many!" I tell them.

That night at home, Papa agrees with me about too many numbers.

He sits at his desk and closes the checkbook and stacks the bills.

"When all the numbers in the world gang up and land on you,

punching and crunching," says Papa, "it's called a math crash!"

"How do you fix math crashes?" I ask.

"I run around the house ten times and take a hot bath,

and they go away," Papa answers.

Weather Watcher

Outside our class window is a thermometer.

Inside the tiny tube the red goes up and down.

"The red goes all high-up and happy on warm days,"

says Miss Cribbage.

"But when the wind blows cold,

the red shrinks down to a little drop."

I am the Weather Watcher.

My job is to copy the thermometer line numbers

onto the weather calendar.

I make a picture of rain or sunshine

just like the weather map

in Papa's newspaper.

50°F

10°C

72°F

22°C

30°F

-1°C

20°F

-7°C

Two Signs

"This sign ? means *I do not know*," Miss Cribbage says.

"We write a question mark every time we don't know the answer."

Miss Cribbage writes another new sign!

"It's the mark that means *Wow!* or *Do it now!*

Roger starts to write question marks and Wow signs all over

the blackboard.

"Those signs belong

to me!" says Roger.

"They are my signs!"

He even draws them

on his shirt.

Precious Stones

In my attic hiding place there is an old trunk.
In it is a lady's fancy hat with pearls
and small spotted feathers.
I have all I need to make
a beautiful present for Mama's birthday.
I spell my mama's name in
diamonds and pearls on the top of an empty tin.
When the box is dry and wrapped,
I put it on her pillow.
Miss Cribbage says the best gifts
are the ones you make.

How Did Music Come Into the World?

Papa plays me my good-night song on his harmonica.

"How did music come into the world?" I want to know.

"Before there was music there was rain," says Papa,

"and wind and fire crackling. Those sounds were

the first music. One night long, long ago, there was a little girl,

and her papa was putting her to sleep.

There was no rain and no wind and no fire, and she could not

go to sleep without them.

So her papa made a harp to sound like the rain.

He carved a flute out of a piece of wood to sound like the wind

in the trees, and he made castanets to sound like the fire

in the fireplace.

And he played them all, and his little girl went to sleep."

"Is that a true story?" I ask my papa.

"As true as any story that ever was."

"Play me one more!" I beg Papa.

"Just a very short one," says Papa.

Our Orchestra

We are practicing "Ode to Joy"
for our spring concert.
It sounds like this

Zizza zizza twee twee
Pung, pung . . . *binga binga*
Shuffle shuffle shuffle shuffle
Ding dong ding.

Diane Duck cannot hit the
triangle at the right moment.

So Miss Cribbage switches Diane
to the rice shufflers and gives
Louise the triangle.

On Monday, Miss Cribbage changes
Diane to the bells.
But Diane Duck rings them at just
the wrong moment.

Diane won't talk on the way home
from school.
"I'm no good at anything!" she says.
We sit in the garden together.

The wind chimes go *dingle tingle*
in the apple tree.
"I have an idea!"
I tell Diane.

On concert night we are
ready for "Ode to Joy"!

On top of Miss Cribbage's piano
is an electric fan.
Diane stands in the breeze of the electric
fan and holds her wind chime up.
It is never out of rhythm.
It is always perfect.

"The tingling and dingling of the wind chimes are the sound of diamond rings gleaming with happiness!" says Diane Duck.

Poetry Day

All the way through jumping rope,
I say it.
All the way home in the bus, I say it.
All the way through picking flowers for
our kitchen table,
I say it.

"Emily!" says my sister, Eloise.
"What are you whispering?"
"I have a poetry recital," I answer.
"I am learning a poem."
Next Friday, everyone in my class
will say their poem.

Early, early in the morning

I say it perfectly in bed.

But when I go to school

I am afraid to say it out loud.

When it is my turn, I open my mouth.

Nothing comes out.

Then I hear a voice.

It is my voice saying it.

Everyone claps.

I run and sit on Mama's lap

and hide my face because

I can't believe I said it,

without missing a word.

with silver buttons all down her back

World of Wonders

We are old enough to go from our school library to
the big library in town.

We get our Cranberry Island library cards.

Each of us picks a book to take home.

Miss Cribbage reads us a story about Aladdin and the Magic Lamp.

Roger says Aladdin has a magic carpet rolled up in the back
of his Cadillac convertible.

"Why does Aladdin need the magic carpet and a car, too?"
asks Martha.

"If Aladdin ever runs out of gas," explains Roger,
"he can jump on his carpet and fly right home
to his mama and papa and his dogs."

The library is our world of wonders.

The Clouds

Some clouds fill with sunshine
Some are dark with sorrow.
Some are left from yesterday
And some are for tomorrow.

The clouds go proudly sailing by.
I love their proper names.

Stratus, Nimbus, Cirrus,
Cumulus, and James.

Cirrus

Cumulus

Stratus and Nimbus

James

78

Miss Maria's Jam

Our big store sells strawberry jam.

But we don't buy our jam from the store.

We buy strawberry jam from Miss Maria's

at the farmers' market.

"It's important," says my mama,

"to buy what our neighbors grow and make.

We help them, and they help us."

So all our milk comes from the farm over

the hill and our eggs from next door.

Some things we buy from far away, because they don't

grow here.

I tell Mama that orange juice comes from Florida

and pineapples from Hawaii.

Here are some things from far away.

Rice from Japan

Orange Juice from Florida

Pineapple from Hawaii

Peanuts from Georgia

Chocolate from Belize

Coffee from Kenya

Dance of the Flowers

"We want the flowers to come out!" shouts Louise.
So we plan a Spring Dance, with spring music.
We make such beautiful spring music that the crocuses and
daffodils will *have* to come out.

Measuring Mania

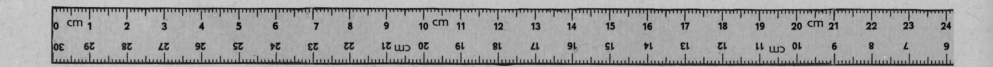

Diana Duck measures with her ruler.

"My daddy's feet are big! They are nine inches long," says Diane.

"My feet are small. They are only four inches long."

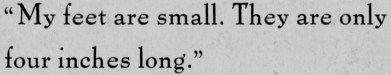

Odysseus brings in a caterpillar.
The caterpillar is very little.
It measures five centimeters long.

Diane pedals her car from house to mailbox.
It is not far. "Twenty meters," says Diane's daddy.

"What's a very faraway thing in the whole wide world?" asks Diane.

"From here to the moon is 238,606 miles!" says Diane's daddy.

Louise measures time.

Louise gets up at seven o'clock.

Louise eats her breakfast in fifteen minutes.

She gets dressed and ready for school in half an hour.

It takes fifteen minutes to get to school. It is now eight o'clock. From bed to breakfast to school takes Louise one hour.

SUN	MON	TUE	WED	THU	FRI	SAT
7	8	9	10	11	12	13

Days in a Week

A week is seven days long.
Today, the ninth of May, is
Louise's birthday.

THE STAR

WEEKLY SINCE 1885

SUN	MON	TUE	WED	THU	FRI	SAT
	1	2	3	4	5	6
7	8	9	10	11	12	13
14	15	16	17	18	19	20
21	22	23	24	25	26	27
28	29	30	31			

Months in a Year

There are twelve months in a year.
Every twelve months, Louise will be
one year older.

Louise is five years old. And today is her birthday all day long.

One Year Old

Two Years Old

Three Years Old

Four Years Old

Five Years Old
Happy Birthday!

Roger and his Dad make chocolate pancakes
on Saturday morning.

Roger measures a cup of milk

and a cup of pancake mix for his dad.

They add six ounces of chocolate.

Roger helps his dad take care of the car.

They drive to the garage and fill up with ten gallons of gas.

Roger's dad drives at the speed limit—30 miles per hour.

"Let's go fast!" says Roger.

"No!" says Roger's dad. "If I go faster, the policeman

will give me a speeding ticket!"

"What's left to measure?" asks Miss Cribbage.

I raise my hand.

"My aunt Mim's blood pressure!" I say.

"It goes up every time she reads a scary story."

Money

Every week I get twenty-five cents allowance.

I have pennies, nickels, dimes, and quarters.

In four weeks, I save up one dollar.

I leave one quarter in my piggy bank.

Grandpa takes me to the store.

He buys groceries.

I buy fake nails for Eloise, Bubble Trouble for Leo,

and a magic ring for me.

Grandpa and I put my last quarter in the Animal Rescue tin.

We have saved.

We have bought what we need.

We have given to others.

Clean-up Day

We go on beaches, fields, and roads,

and we pick up all the trash.

Everyone cheers for our Biggest Bag winner, Odysseus.

Anyone who leaves a mess in our classroom

has to stay after school to clean up.

"I wish the world was like Miss Cribbage's room!"

says Diane Duck.

Miss Cribbage tells us, "Your job is to grow up and make those

rules for everyone. Then the world will be a cleaner place!"

90

Adopting Great-granny

On Cranberry Island, there is a big old house.

In the house are many great-grannies and great-grandpas

whose families live far away.

Each of us adopts a great-grandpa or a great-granny.

We play cards with our adopted great-grannies and -grandpas.

We sing songs, listen to stories, and learn things

like making a cat's cradle.

Each week we bring a present.

My adopted great-granny is almost a hundred years old.

She has forgotten her name.

She and I picked a new one.

We decided on *Starlight*.

Star light, star bright is the song she remembers best.

"Promise to come back!" says Starlight.

"Oh, yes!" I say. "Mama is making maple candy this week.

She lets me help. I will bring you maple candy next time."

Maple candy is Starlight's favorite in the world.

The Last Day of School

On the playground we have a secret vote on our good-bye present to Miss Cribbage.

Otto nominates ice cream.

Martha thinks we should all chip in and buy Miss Cribbage a pair of blue shoes because she doesn't have that color.

I learned to add.

I learned to play a musical instrument.

Here is my portrait of Miss Cribbage.

I cleaned up the beach.

Diane Duck says, "Let's make her pictures
of our favorite things we learned in kindergarten
so that she can keep them forever and ever
and hang them on the wall."
Diane Duck's idea carries the day.

I discovered poetry.

I learned new
holidays.

POE
M

I learned names
of leaves.

I learned to drive.

Miss Cribbage's
List of Important
Words to Recognize:

A, am, an, and, are, at, ate,
big, by, can, come, did, for,
go, got, had, has, he, here,
I, in, is, it, let, like, look,
me, my, no, not, or, see,
she, so, the, this, to, up,
was, went, you.